HANDS-ON HISTORY

FASHION

BRING THE PAST ALIVE WITH 30 GREAT PROJECTS

Consulting editors Rachel Halstead and Struan Reid

southwater

This edition is published by Southwater

Southwater is an imprint of Anness Publishing Ltd
Hermes House, 88–89 Blackfriars Road, London SE1 8HA
tel. 020 7401 2077; fax 020 7633 9499
www.southwaterbooks.com; info@anness.com
© Anness Publishing Ltd 2003

This edition distributed in the UK by The Manning Partnership Ltd
tel. 01225 478 444; fax 01225 478 440
sales@manning-partnership.co.uk

This edition distributed in the USA and Canada by National
Book Network
tel. 301 459 3366; fax 301 459 1705
www.nbnbooks.com

This edition distributed in Australia by Pan Macmillan Australia
tel. 1300 135 113; fax 1300 135 103;
customer.service@macmillan.com.au

This edition distributed in New Zealand by The Five Mile Press
(NZ) Ltd
tel. (09) 444 4144; fax (09) 444 4518;
fivemilenz@clear.net.nz

Publisher: Joanna Lorenz
Managing Editor: Linda Fraser
Editors: Leon Gray, Sarah Uttridge
Designer: Sandra Marques/Axis Design Editions Ltd
Jacket Design: Dean Price
Photographers: Paul Bricknell and John Freeman
Illustrators: Rob Ashby, Julian Baker, Andy Beckett, Mark Beesley,
Mark Bergin, Richard Berridge, Peter Bull Art Studio, Vanessa Card,
Stuart Carter, Rob Chapman, James Field, Wayne Ford, Chris Forsey,
Mike Foster, Terry Gabbey, Roger Gorringe, Jeremy Gower, Peter
Gregory, Stephen Gyapay, Ron Hayward, Gary Hincks, Sally Holmes,
Richard Hook, Rob Jakeway, John James, Kuo Chen Kang, Aziz Khan,
Stuart Lafford, Ch'en Ling, Steve Lings, Kevin Maddison, Janos
Marffy, Shane Marsh, Rob McCaig, Chris Odgers, Alex Pang, Helen
Parsley, Terry Riley, Andrew Robinson, Chris Rothero, Eric Rowe,
Martin Sanders, Peter Sarson, Mike Saunders, Rob Sheffield, Guy
Smith, Don Simpson, Donato Spedaliere, Nick Spender, Clive
Spong, Stuart Squires, Roger Stewart, Sue Stitt, Ken Stott, Steve
Sweet, Mike Taylor, Alisa Tingley, Catherine Ward, Shane Watson,
Ross Watton, Alison Winfield, John Whetton, Mike White, Stuart
Wilkinson, John Woodcock
Stylists: Jane Coney, Konika Shakar, Thomasina Smith,
Melanie Williams

Previously published as part of a larger compendium, *120 Great
History Projects*.
Picture credits: Bryan and Cherry Alexander: 21bl, 26bl; The Art
Archive:32tr, 46t; Christies Images: 46b; The Hutchison Library: 31t/Robert
Francis, 88b; South American Pictures/Diego Rivera: 31b.

10 9 8 7 6 5 4 3 2 1

Contents

Mesoamerican workers making accessories with feathers

Fashion and Accessories

Some clothes are made for work and comfort, while others are designed to show how important the wearer is. Jewellery and other accessories, such as headwear, are often a sign of the wearer's wealth. This book looks at the practical clothes worn by people through the ages. It also examines the distinctive styles, fashions and materials adopted by different cultures throughout the world.

Fashion and Clothing

U nlike animals and birds, humans do not have fur and feathers to keep them warm. One of the main reasons we wear clothes is to protect ourselves from the weather, the Sun as well as the cold. However, clothes are much more than just a form of protection. They have long been used as statements about the people who wear them. Special clothes worn by different groups of people indicated their position in society, their religious beliefs or the sort of work they did. From the very earliest times, people also cared about how they looked. So they decorated their clothes with shells and beads, and coloured threads were woven together to produce brightly patterned materials.

▲ The first clothing

Animals were hunted by early people not only for their meat but also for their skins. These were scraped clean and shaped with sharp stone tools. Later methods of treating the skins made them soft and supple and therefore comfortable to wear.

◄ Cool, crisp linen

The clothes worn by the ancient Greeks were simple and elegant. The most common piece of clothing was a loose linen tunic. This was cool and comfortable to wear during the hot summer months.

◂ Wedding clothes

The Aztec people of Mexico wore clothes made of cotton. Here a man and woman are shown in their wedding outfits. Their cloaks have been tied together to show that the couple are now bound together in marriage.

▾ Rich embroidery

This picture shows the Hindu god Brahma wearing red pantaloons and a gold hat. The woman to the left is wearing a traditional Indian form of dress called a sari. The clothes are very simple, but they are made from beautifully embroidered silk, which indicates the importance of the people wearing them.

◂ A warrior's clothes

The samurai were an elite warrior class of old Japan. The formal clothes of a samurai were called *kami-shimo*. They showed his high status. The outfit consisted of a winged jacket, known as a *kataginu,* with matching trousers, called *hakama,* worn over a long tunic called a *kimono.*

Stone Age dyed cloth

The hunters of the last Ice Age were the first people to wear clothes to protect them from the cold. They sewed animal hides together with strips of leather. The first clothes included simple trousers, tunics and cloaks, decorated with beads of coloured stones, teeth and shells. Fur boots were stitched together with leather laces.

Furs were prepared by stretching out the hides and scraping them clean. The clothes were cut out and holes were made around the edges of the pieces with a sharp, pointed stone called an awl. This made it easier to pass a bone needle through the hide. Cleaned hides were also used to make tents, bags and bedding. After sheep were domesticated in the Near East, wool was used to weave cloth. Plant fibres, such as flax, cotton, bark and cactus, were used elsewhere. The cloth was coloured and decorated with plant dyes.

oak bark

dyer's broom

birch bark

▲ Nature's colours
Stone Age people used the flowers, stems, bark and leaves of many plants to make brightly coloured dyes.

▼ Mammoth shelter
During most of the last 100,000 years, the Earth's climate has been much colder than it is today. Stone Age people dressed warmly. Their clothes kept out the cold and the rain.

YOU WILL NEED

Natural dyes (such as walnuts, elderberries and safflower), tablespoon, saucepan, pestle and mortar, water, sieve, bowl, old white cloth or chamois leather, rubber gloves (optional), white card, white T-shirt, wooden spoon. (Many natural dyes can be found in good health food shops.)

1 Choose your first dye and put between 8 and 12 tablespoons of the dye into an old saucepan. You may need to crush or shred the dye with a pestle and mortar.

2 Cover the dye with water and ask an adult to bring it to the boil and then simmer for one hour. Leave it to cool. Pour the dye through a sieve into a bowl to remove the lumps.

3 Test the dye using a piece of cloth or chamois leather. Dip the cloth into the dye for a few minutes. You could wear rubber gloves to stop any dye getting on to your hands.

4 Lay the cloth or chamois leather patch on to a piece of white card and leave it to dry. Be careful not to drip the dye over clothes or upholstery while you work.

5 Make up the two other dyes and test them out in the same way. When all three pieces of cloth or leather are dry, compare the patches and choose your favourite colour.

6 Dye a white T-shirt by preparing it in your chosen dye. Try to make sure that the T-shirt is dyed evenly all over. Make sure it is completely dry before you try it on.

The bark, leaves and husks of the walnut dyed fabric a deep brown colour. Elderberries gave cloth a rich purple-brown colour. The flowers of the safflower plant were picked when first open, then dried. Fabric dyed with safflower, like this T-shirt, was light brown in colour.

Greek chiton

Clothes were styled simply in ancient Greece. Both men and women wore long tunics. These draped loosely for comfort and were held in place with pins or brooches. Heavy cloaks were worn for travelling or in bad weather. Clothes were made of home-spun wool and linen. Fabrics were coloured with dyes made from plants, insects and shellfish.

cotton

linen

Only the wealthiest Greeks wore clothes made from cotton or linen. Poorer citizens wore clothes made from home-spun wool.

YOU WILL NEED

Tape measure, rectangle of cloth – the width should measure the same as the height of your shoulder, scissors, pins, chalk, needle, thread, 12 metal buttons (with loops), cord.

1 Measure your arm span from wrist to wrist and double the figure. Measure your length from shoulder to ankle. Cut your cloth to these figures. Fold the fabric in half widthways.

2 Pin the two sides together. Draw a chalk line across the fabric, 2cm in from the edge. Sew along the line, turn the material inside out and re-fold the fabric so the seam is at the back.

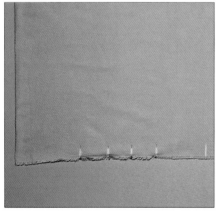

3 At one of the open ends of the fabric, mark a central gap for your head. Pin the fabric together there. From the head gap, mark a point every 5cm to the end of the fabric.

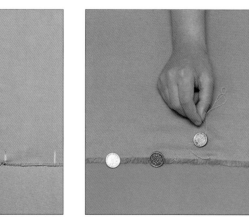

4 Pin together the front and back along these points. At each pin, sew on a button to hold the two sides of fabric together. To secure the button, sew through the loop several times.

Tie the cord around your waist. If it is too long, cut it to the right length, but leave enough cord to tie. Bunch the chiton material up, over the cord.

Roman toga

Most Roman clothes were made of wool that had been spun and woven by hand at home or in a workshop. The most common style of clothing was the tunic, which was practical for active people such as workers and slaves. Important men also wore a garment called a toga. This was a 6m length of cloth with a curved edge, wrapped around the body and draped over the shoulder.

◄ A change in colour

Roman women wore a long dress called a stola over an under-tunic. Only married women wore dresses dyed in bright colours. Girls dressed in white.

YOU WILL NEED

Double-sided sticky tape, purple ribbon, old white sheet, scissors, long T-shirt, cord.

1 Use double-sided sticky tape to stick the ribbon along the long edge of the sheet. Cut one corner off as shown. Put on a long white T-shirt tied at the waist with a cord.

2 Get a friend to hold the long edge of the fabric behind you. The cut corner should be on your left hand side. Drape about a quarter of the toga over your left arm and shoulder.

3 Bring the rest of the toga round to the front, passing it under your right arm. Hook the toga up by tucking a few folds of the material securely into the cord around your waist.

4 Now your friend can help you fold the rest of the toga neatly over your left arm, as shown above. If you prefer, you could drape it over your left shoulder.

Boys from wealthy families wore togas edged with a thin purple stripe until they reached the age of 16. Then they wore plain togas.

Indian sari

Clothing has always been very simple in India. Noble people, both men and women, usually wore a single piece of fabric that was draped around the hips, drawn up between the legs and then fastened securely again at the waist. Women wore bodices above the waist, but men were often bare-chested. Although their clothes were simple, people had elaborate hairstyles with flowers and other decorations. Men and women also wore a lot of jewellery, such as earrings, armbands, breastplates, nose rings and anklets. The Hindu male garment was called the dhoti, and the female garment gradually evolved into the sari – a single large cloth draped around the body, with a bodice worn underneath.

▲ A guide for the gods

A Brahmin (priest) looks after the temple and is a go-between for the worshipper and a god. He wears a sacred cotton cord across his chest to symbolize his position.

◄ Noble warriors

Society in ancient India was divided into three castes (classes). The noble warrior class (Kshatriya) was the next highest class after the Brahmin. Noble warriors wore expensive jewellery and used weapons such as bows and arrows, daggers, spears and swords.

▼ Holy water

Hindus have bathed in the sacred River Ganges for centuries. The religion states that bathing in its waters washes away sin. People wear their dhotis or saris when they bathe.

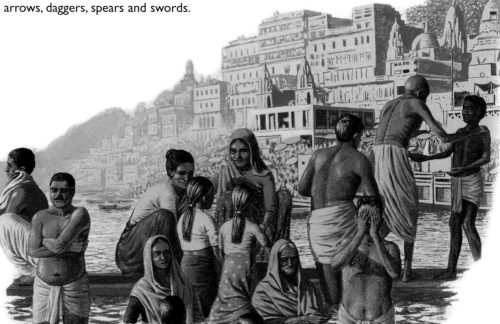

YOU WILL NEED

Silky or cotton fabric measuring 4 x 1m, one large safety pin. Dip a cork into gold paint and press it along one long edge of the fabric to add decoration to the sari. Leave to dry before trying it on.

1 Hold one corner of the fabric to your stomach with the decorated border on the outside. Wrap the long side of the fabric once tightly around your waist.

2 Make a number of pleats where the fabric comes back around to the front of your body. Make them as even as you can. The pleats act as the underskirt of your sari.

3 Tuck the pleated section of the sari into the waist of the underskirt. You could use a safety pin to hold the pleats in place, while you practise tying the sari.

4 Take the excess length of fabric in your left hand and pass it all the way around your back. Take extra care that the pleats do not come out.

A sari is a single large cloth that covers both the upper and the lower body. Saris were first worn in eastern India over 1,000 years ago.

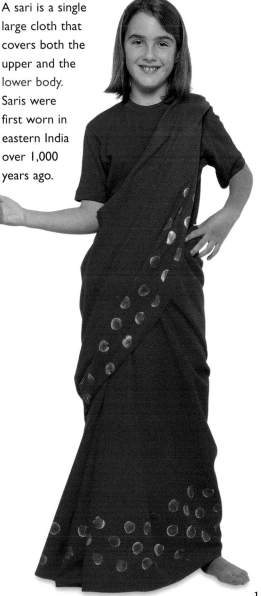

5 Now take the rest of the sari fabric in your right hand and lift it up so that it is level with your shoulders. Do this in front of a mirror if possible, so that you can see what you are doing.

6 Swing the fabric over your left shoulder. The fabric should fall in gentle folds from your shoulder, across your body to the level of your waist. You may need to practise doing this.

Native American robe

The clothes of most Native Americans were made from the skins of bison (American buffalo). Hunters performed elaborate dances before a hunt, and then headed off in search of animal tracks. Early hunters stalked the animals on foot, often disguised as other animals. Later, horses made the job a lot easier. Once the bison was killed, women and elder children usually processed the carcass. The skin was taken off in one piece and used to make clothes and covers. Meat was prepared for a feast to celebrate the successful hunt.

YOU WILL NEED

Three pieces of an old bed sheet (one measuring 140 x 60cm and the other two measuring 40 x 34cm), pencil, tape measure, scissors, large needle, brown thread, felt (red, yellow, dark blue and light blue are the best colours to use), PVA glue and glue brush, black embroidery thread, red thread.

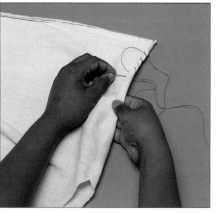

1 Fold the larger piece of fabric in half for the body. Draw and cut a curved neckline 22 x 6cm on the fold. Roll the fabric over at the shoulders and stitch it down with brown thread.

2 Open the body fabric out flat and line up the two smaller fabric rectangles for the arm pieces with the centre of the stitched ridge. Stitch the top edge of the pieces on to the body.

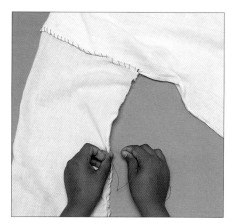

3 Fold the fabric in half again to see the shirt's shape. Now stitch up the undersides of the sleeves. (Native Americans did not usually sew the sides of skin robes together.)

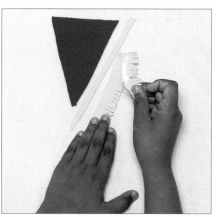

4 Your shirt is ready to decorate. Cut out strips and triangles of coloured felt and glue them on to the shirt. Make decorative fringes by cutting into one side of strips of felt.

5 Make fake hair strips by cutting 8cm lengths of black embroidery thread and tying them in bunches. Tie red thread tightly around the top, and then glue the fake hair on to your shirt.

Native Americans made their clothes from young bison, and the resulting animal hide was called buckskin.

Inca tunic

The standard of Inca weaving was very high. The Inca people had to weave cloth for the state as a form of tax, and woven cloth was often used to pay officials. Inca men wore a loincloth around the waist, secured by a belt. Over this was a knee-length tunic, often made of alpaca – a fine, silky wool. Women wrapped themselves in a large, rectangular piece of alpaca.

◀ **Fighting force**
Inca warriors decorated their war dress with brightly coloured feathers.

YOU WILL NEED

40cm square of red felt, 160 x 65cm rectangle of blue felt, PVA glue and glue brush, tape measure, scissors, needle and thread, pencil, ruler, cream calico fabric, fabric paints, paintbrush, water pot.

1 Place the blue felt flat on the table with the long side facing towards you. Position the red felt in the centre of the blue felt to form a diamond. Glue the red felt in place here.

2 Cut a 22cm-long slit through the centre of both felt layers. Fold the fabric along the slit. Cut a 12cm-long slit through one double layer of fabric at right angles to the first slit as shown.

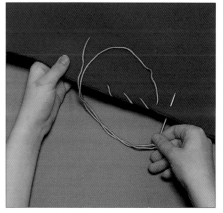

3 Use the needle and thread to sew together the sides of the tunic. Make the stitches as large as possible and be sure to leave enough space for armholes at the top.

4 Draw lots of 5cm squares in pencil on the cream calico fabric. Paint on colourful designs like the ones shown and leave them to dry. Cut out the squares and glue them to your tunic.

When the glue is dry you can try on your tunic. The original Inca tunics were brightly coloured and decorated with geometric patterns.

Medieval witch

The familiar image of a witch – dressed in ragged clothes with a broomstick and a warty face – developed from a much-feared folklore figure called the hag. Myths, from ancient Egypt through to pre-Christian Europe, tell of ugly old women who used supernatural power to bring misfortune to those around them. During medieval times, many innocent old women who looked like hags became the victims of witch hunts. They were tried and usually found guilty, then sentenced to burn alive at the stake.

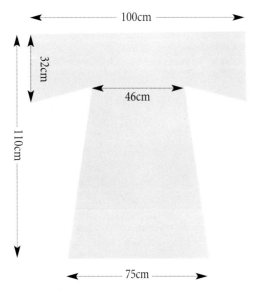

100cm
32cm
46cm
110cm
75cm

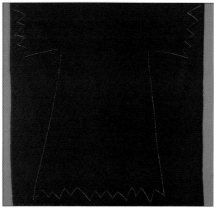

1 Fold the black fabric in half widthways. Lay it out on a flat surface. Then use the template to draw the witch's dress shape on to the fabric with a white pencil.

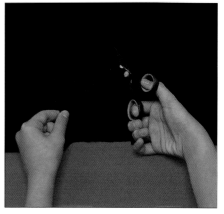

2 Cut out the dress shape. Cut a slit 24cm across in the middle of the folded edge for your neck. Then cut a second line 12cm long down the back of the fabric.

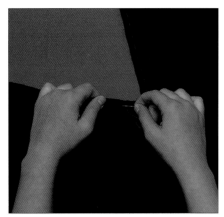

3 Turn the fabric inside out. Use a needle and some thread to sew a simple running stitch up each side of the witch's dress. Then sew under the arms of the dress.

4 Cut a jagged edge along the cuffs of each sleeve and along the bottom of the dress. Turn the dress inside out so that the fabric is right side out and the stitches are hidden.

5 Lay the dress on a sheet of old newspaper. Dip a stiff brush in silver paint. Pull the bristles back towards you and spray paint on to the fabric. When dry, spray the other side.

6 Roll the rectangle of thin, black card into the shape of a cone. Use a white pencil to draw a shape on the card to show where it overlaps and should be taped.

7 Cut away the excess card and roll the card back into a cone shape. Then secure it with sticky tape. Trim the bottom edge of the cone to fit the size of your head.

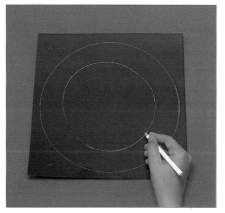

8 Place the hat on the square black card. Use the white pencil to draw a rough circle around the rim about 5cm away from it. Draw a second circle to fit exactly around the rim of the hat.

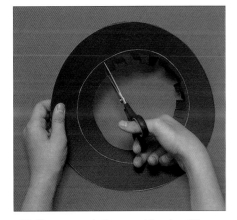

9 Cut around the outside ring. Then cut out the centre, making sure to leave an extra 3cm inside the white line ring. Make snips into the ring as far as the line to make small tabs.

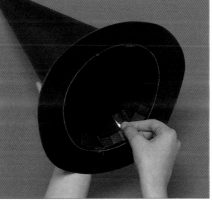

10 Fit the rim of the hat on to the bottom of the cone-shaped section. Fold the tabs up inside the hat and use small pieces of sticky tape to fix the rim to the hat.

11 Draw a rectangular shape on to the silver card to make a hat buckle. Draw a second rectangle inside the first one. Cut out the buckle and glue it on to the front of the hat.

12 Cut sheets of green and black tissue into long strips to make witch's hair. Glue the strips all the way around the inside of the witch's hat, leaving a gap at the front by the buckle.

Complete the witch's look by using face paints. Paint dark lines under your eyes and around your mouth to make you look as if you have wrinkles. Black out one of your teeth. You will also need a broom, which you can make by tying twigs to an old broom handle.

Cowboy gear

The clothes of a typical cowboy had to be tough, because he spent a long time in the saddle. Overtrousers called chaps protected his legs from the cattle's horns, as well as from burn marks from throwing his lassos. High-heeled leather boots helped to keep the rider's feet in the stirrups on the saddle. The cowboy's hat was usually made from a type of hard-wearing wool called felt. A wide brim shielded his face from the sun. Hats could also double up as water carriers for horses to drink from.

Leg chaps

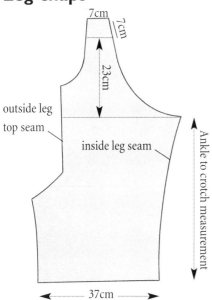

7cm
7cm
23cm
outside leg top seam
inside leg seam
Ankle to crotch measurement
37cm

1 Cut two templates from paper. Fold the fabric in half to make a long thin piece with the right sides together. Pin the templates to the material. Cut round the fabric to make four pieces.

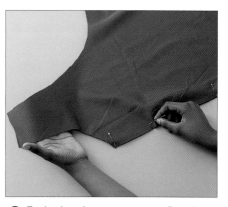

2 Each chap has two pieces. Pin the outside leg top seam of one of the chaps as shown. Use a running stitch to sew 1.5cm in from the cut edge. Pin and sew the inside leg seam.

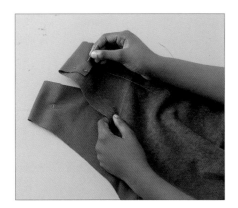

3 Turn the leg the right way out. Following the top dotted line on the template, fold over the belt loops. Pin them along the bottom edge and then carefully stitch them.

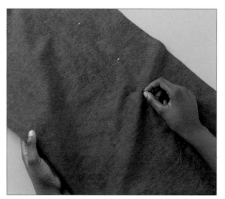

4 Pin and then sew the outside part of the outside leg bottom seam 10cm in from the cut edge. Make your stitches as neat as possible, as they will be visible when you wear the chaps.

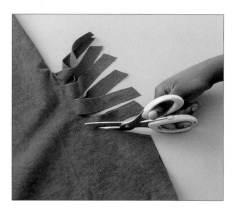

5 Cut strips into the wide flap down the outside leg to make a fringe. Try not to cut into the seam. Repeat steps 1 to 6 to make the second leg for your chaps.

Felt hat

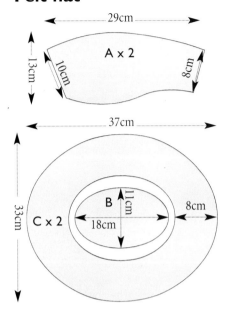

1 Make the templates from paper and pin them to the felt. Cut out. Pin and sew the two short sides of the hat (template A). Pin and sew the crown (template B) to the top of the sides.

2 Take template C and pin it on to the piece of stiffened fabric. Cut around it, and then cut out the hole in the centre. The result will be used to make the brim of your cowboy hat.

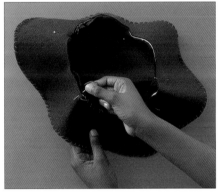

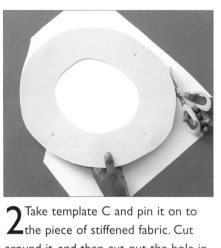

3 Sandwich the stiffened fabric between the two felt brims cut using template C and pin the two sides of the brim together. Sew the outside edge of all three pieces as shown.

4 Turn the hat brim upside down and carefully pin it to the hat crown you have just made. This way, the seam will end up inside the hat. Sew the pieces together as shown above.

To put on your chaps, pull each leg over your jeans. Then get someone to help you thread a thick leather belt through the loops front and back. Don't forget your hat and 'kerchief!

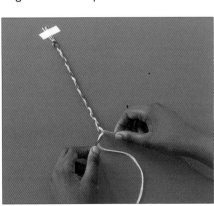

5 Cut 1m lengths from each of the three balls of coloured wool. Fold each strand of wool in half. Knot them at the top and tape them to a work surface. Then plait the wool together.

6 Finish the plait by tying a knot at each end. The plait will become the decorative band for your hat when you wrap it around the base of the crown and knot it tightly around the rim.

Hats and Headwear

Hats and headwear have been worn by men and women all over the world for thousands of years. Their original purpose was to protect the head from extremes of weather, but hats also became signs of status or official position. A crown came to indicate the authority of a king or queen, while religious and military leaders wore headgear that readily identified them and the position they held. As fashion accessories, hats and headwear have been made in bright colours, beautiful materials and all sorts of shapes. They have been decorated with feathers, beads, jewels and bows.

▲ Sun worshipper

Pharaoh Akhenaten of Egypt, shown worshipping the sun god Aten, wore a number of different crowns to indicate his many different roles as ruler of Egypt. Here, Akhenaten wears a special type of hat to show his position as high priest.

◄ A band of gold

Boudicca, queen of the Iceni tribe in Celtic Britain, wears a gold band around her head. This band is called a diadem and indicates her important position as a ruler. Rare and precious gold was considered to be the metal of royalty.

Imperial silk ▲

Puyi, the last emperor of China, ascended to the throne as a small boy. He wears richly embroidered silk robes and a small silk skullcap decorated with coloured embroidery.

▲ Mayan splendour

A mural shows two warriors from Central America standing over a captive. They wear the magnificent clothes of the Mayan nobility. The headdresses, decorated with feathers and even an animal head, indicate the importance of the two warriors.

▲ Practical headwear

A Saami boy from Lapland wears a traditional pom-pom hat. It is a cheerful and very practical design for the Arctic climate.

◀ European adventurer

A Portuguese naval officer from the early 1600s wears the typical clothes of his high social position. On his head he wears a small, neat hat called a copotain, which has a narrow brim and is made of fur or felt.

Egyptian crown

The pharaohs of ancient Egypt wore many accessories to show that they were important. Pictures and statues showed them with special badges of royalty, such as crowns, headcloths, false beards, sceptres and a crook and flail held in each hand.

The word pharaoh comes from the Egyptian *per-aa* (great house or palace). Later, the word came to mean the person, or ruler, who lived in the palace. The pharaoh was the most important person in Egypt and the link between the people and their gods. The Egyptians believed that on his death, the pharaoh became a god in his own right.

The pharaoh led a busy life. He was the high priest, the chief law-maker, the commander of the army and in charge of the country's wealth. He had to be a clever politician, too. Generally, pharaohs were men, but queens could rule if a male successor was too young. A pharaoh could take several wives. In a royal family, it was common for fathers to marry daughters and for brothers to marry sisters. Sometimes, however, pharaohs married foreign princesses to make an alliance with another country.

▲ Royal headwear
Thutmose III is remembered as a brave warrior king. This picture shows him wearing the headcloth that is one of the special symbols of royalty.

Templates

▲ Crowning glory
Rameses III was the last great warrior pharaoh. Here, Rameses is wearing an elaborate crown that is another special badge of royalty.

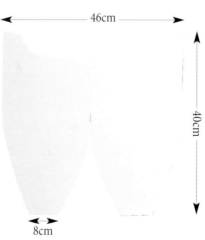

46cm

40cm

8cm

White crown of Upper Egypt

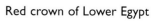
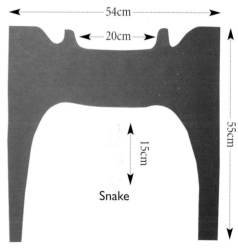

54cm

20cm

15cm

55cm

Snake

Red crown of Lower Egypt

YOU WILL NEED

Two large sheets of card (red and white), pencil, ruler, scissors, masking tape, cardboard roll, bandage, tennis ball, PVA glue and glue brush, white and gold acrylic paints, water pot, paintbrush, beads, skewer.

1 Make each section of the crown using the templates. Bend the white crown section into a cylinder. Use lengths of masking tape to join the two edges of the cylinder together.

The double crown worn by the pharaohs was called the *pschent*. It symbolized the unification of the two kingdoms. The white section at the top (the *hedjet*) stood for Upper Egypt. The red section at the bottom (the *deshret*) stood for Lower Egypt.

2 Tape the cardboard roll into the hole at the top of your pharaoh's crown. Plug the end of the crown with bandages or a tennis ball wedged in position and glue down the edges.

3 Wrap the white section of the crown with lengths of bandage. Paint over these with an equal mixture of white paint and glue. Leave the crown in a warm place to dry.

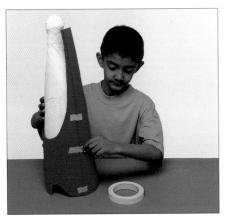

4 Now take the red crown section. Wrap it tightly around the white crown section as shown above. Hold the two sections together using strips of masking tape.

5 Paint the snake shape with gold acrylic paint and stick on beads for its eyes. When dry, score lines across its body with a skewer. Bend the body and glue it to the front of the crown.

Tribal headdress

One of the most popular images of a Native American is that of a warrior dressed in fringed buckskin and a war bonnet, and decorated with body paint and beads. That was just one style of dress, mainly used by the Plains tribes. A warrior had to earn the right to wear a headdress like the one you can make in this project. Each act of bravery during conflict earned the warrior the right to tie another feather to his headdress. Plains warriors also tied locks of their victims' hair to the front of their shirts.

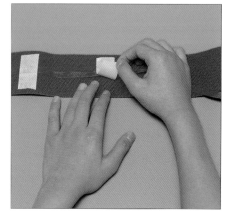

1 Lay the 1m-long red ribbon along the middle of the upholstery tape. Leave 12.5cm lengths at each end to tie the headdress on. Tape the ribbon on to the upholstery tape and sew it on.

2 Cut 26 feather shapes from the white paper, each 18cm long and 4cm wide. Paint the tips black. When the paint is dry, make tiny cuts around the edges of the paper feathers.

3 Cut the balsa dowelling into 26 lengths, each 14cm long. Carefully glue the dowelling to the centre of the back of each feather, starting just below the painted black tip.

4 Take the six real bird feathers and tie them with cotton thread on to the bottom of six of the feathers you made earlier. These will be at the front of the headdress.

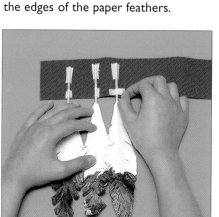

5 Glue and tape all the feathers on to the front of the red band, overlapping the feathers slightly as you go. Position them so that the six real feathers are in the centre.

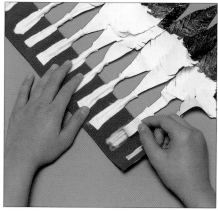

6 Measure and cut 26 lengths of white felt. Each piece of felt should be 6 x 1cm. Glue the felt strips over each piece of balsa dowelling, so that the sticks are hidden.

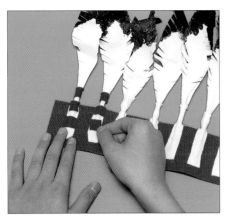

7 Cut out red felt pieces measuring 1.5 x 1cm. Cut three pieces for five feathers at each end and two pieces for the rest. Glue the red felt on to the white felt to make stripes.

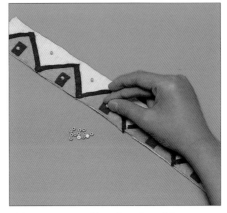

8 Cut out a 40 x 4cm band from yellow felt. Glue on triangles of dark blue and light blue felt and small squares of red felt as shown. You can also decorate it with beads or sequins.

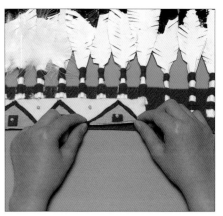

9 Carefully glue the decorative band on to the red band using a ruler to help you place it in the middle. Some feathers will show on either side of the band.

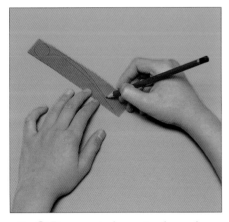

10 Draw a circle on to the red paper, 3cm in diameter. Then draw a 15cm-long tail feather starting at the circle. It should measure 1cm across and taper to a point.

11 Draw seven more of these tail feathers and cut them out. Glue them on to the ends of the feathers on the middle of the band so that the points stick into the air.

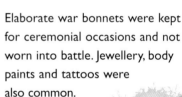

Elaborate war bonnets were kept for ceremonial occasions and not worn into battle. Jewellery, body paints and tattoos were also common.

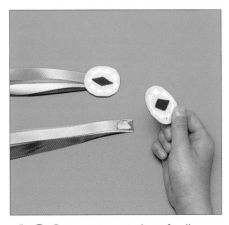

12 Cut out two circles of yellow felt, 5cm in diameter. Decorate the felt circles with red and white felt shapes. Glue coloured ribbons to the backs of the circles.

13 Finally, stick the felt circles on to the headdress on top of the decorative band. The circles should be placed so that the ribbons hang down either side by your ears.

Arctic Saami hat

Clothes in the Arctic were often beautiful as well as practical. Strips or patches of different furs were used to form designs and geometric patterns on outer clothes. Fur trimmings, toggles and other decorative fastenings added final touches to many clothes. Jewellery included pendants, bracelets, necklaces and brooches. Ornaments such as these were traditionally made of natural materials, such as bone and walrus ivory.

Inuit women from North America decorated clothes with birds' beaks, tiny feathers or porcupine quills. In Greenland, lace and glass beads were popular decorations. The clothes of the Saami from Scandinavia were the most colourful. Saami men, women and children wore blue outfits with a red and yellow trim. Men's costumes included tall hats and flared tunics. Women's clothes included flared skirts with embroidered hems and colourful hats, shawls and scarves.

▲ Animal insulation
In the bitter Arctic cold, people wore warm, waterproof clothing made from the skins of animals such as seals.

▲ Colourful costumes
A Saami herdsman in traditional dress holds aloft a reindeer calf born at the end of the spring migration.

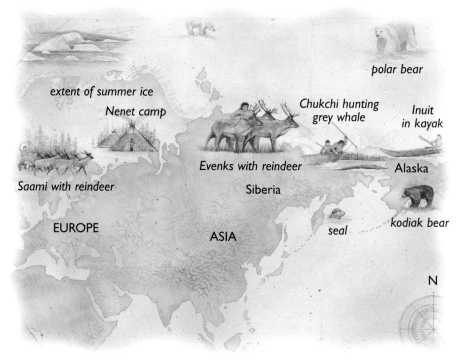

▲ Arctic inhabitants
This map shows some of the main groups of people who still live in the Arctic region. Many Arctic peoples, such as the Saami and Evenks, have long depended on reindeer for food and to make clothes, shelter and tools.

YOU WILL NEED

Red felt measuring 58 x 30cm, ruler, pencil, black ribbon measuring 58 x 2cm, PVA glue and glue brush, coloured ribbon measuring 58cm, white felt measuring 58cm, pair of compasses, red card, scissors, ribbon strips (red, green and white) measuring 44 x 4cm, red ribbon measuring 58 x 4cm.

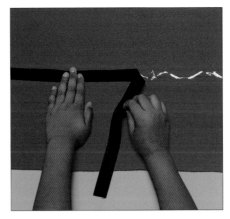

1 Use a ruler and pencil to mark out the centre of the piece of red felt along its length. Carefully glue the length of black ribbon along the centre line as shown above.

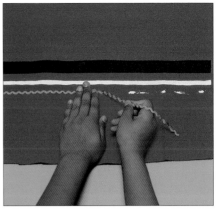

2 Continue to decorate the red felt section with pieces of coloured ribbon. You can add some strips of white felt to add to your striking Saami hat design.

3 Cut out a circle of red card with a diameter of 18cm. Draw a circle inside with a diameter of 15cm. Cut into the larger circle as far as the 15cm line to make a series of tabs.

4 Glue the ends of the decorated red felt section together as shown above. You will need to wrap this felt section around your head and measure it to ensure the hat fits properly.

5 Fold down the tabs cut into the circle of red card. Dab them with glue, tuck them inside one end of the red felt section and then stick them firmly to make the top of the hat.

6 While the hat is drying, glue the coloured ribbon strips together. Glue these strips 15cm from the end of the 58cm-long band of red ribbon. Glue this to the base of the hat.

The style of Saami hats varied from one place to another. In southern Norway, men's hats were tall and rounded. Further north, their hats had four points.

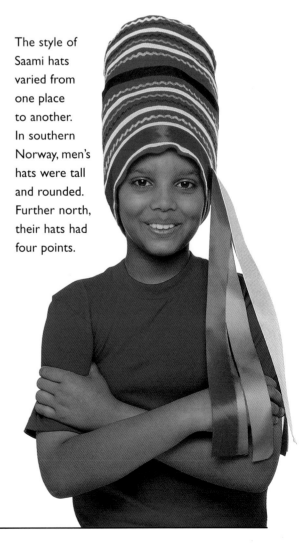

Medieval headpiece

In the Middle Ages, noble ladies hid their hair beneath a fancy headdress. The ring-shaped chaplet you can make in this project is one of the simpler headdress styles worn in medieval times. The more wealthy, fashionable and important a lady was, the more elaborate her clothes were. Some robes were embroidered and trimmed with fur – they were extremely expensive and expected to last a lifetime. Traders came to the castle to present a choice of materials and designs. When the lady had chosen, tailors made the clothes.

▲ **Dressed to impress**
A lady needs help from a maid to put on her complicated headpiece.

YOU WILL NEED

Pencil, ruler, corrugated card, scissors, masking tape, 2m fine fabric, two sponges, 3-4m netting, string, acrylic paints, paintbrush, water pot, nylon stocking, cotton wool, ribbon, needle and thread, 1m gold braid, PVA glue and glue brush, 2 x 2cm silver card, three 7cm lengths of thin wire, beads.

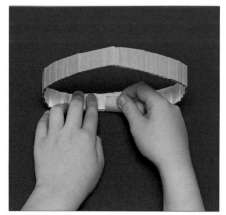

1 Cut a 4cm strip of corrugated card to fit around your head exactly, about 30cm in length. Overlap the ends of the strip and firmly secure them with masking tape.

2 Cut two squares of the fine fabric, each one big enough to wrap around the sponge. Then cut two squares of netting slightly larger than the fabric squares.

3 Lay the fabric squares over the net squares. Place a sponge in the middle of each fabric square. Gather the netting and fabric over the sponges and tie them with string.

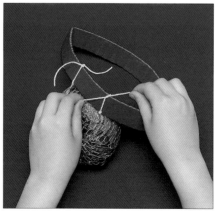

4 Paint the card circle for your head. Thread two lengths of string through each sponge and net ball. Use the string to hang one ball on each side of the card circlet.

5 Cut the bottom half leg off a coloured nylon stocking. Pack the inside tightly with cotton wool to make a firm, full sausage shape. Knot the open end to close it.

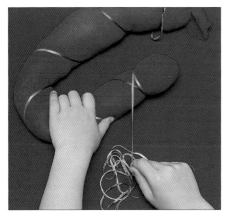

6 Tie the ribbon around one end of the sausage. Wind it diagonally along the sausage and then wind it back again to cross diagonally over the first row.

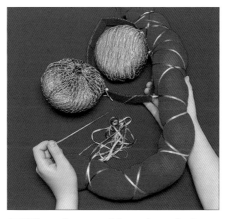

7 Thread more ribbon through the ribbon crossovers on the sausage. Then take the ribbon over and around the head circlet to join the sausage and band together.

8 Sew the two ends of the sausage shape together. Sew one end of the gold braid to cover the join. Then glue the braid around the sausage, as shown.

9 Cut out a flower shape from the 2 x 2cm silver card as shown above. Bend one end of the wire into a hook. Thread some beads on to the other end. Then bend the wire over.

10 Glue the flower shape on to the front of the headdress. Hook the wire beads in the middle. Glue more beads and braid around the headdress.

11 Make a double pleat in the remaining length of fabric to make the veil. Secure the veil to the inside back half of the headdress with masking tape.

A real medieval hat was called a chaplet. It was made of silk or satin fabric and held in place by a hair net. The ring-shaped chaplet fitted on top of a veil, and the veil hung down at the back of the head. Ladies often shaved the hair at the front of their heads to make their foreheads look high. For an authentic medieval look, tuck your hair out of sight under the hat.

Weaving and Sewing

T he very first clothes that people wore were made from tied grasses or tree bark, or the skins of animals. The invention of the sewing needle enabled people to join different pieces of material together. Clothes became more varied and also fitted more comfortably. The weaving loom completely transformed the clothes people wore. Long lengths of cloth could be made into tents, mats and wall hangings, or cut and shaped into clothes. The weaving loom was one of the first pieces of industrial equipment to be used. The earliest known cloth was woven at least 7,000 years ago in what is now Palestine.

▲ Easy weaving

Backstrap looms were first used by the Incas around 2500BC and continue to be used in Central and South America. The upright, or warp, threads are tensioned between an upright post and a beam attached to the weaver's waist. The cross, or weft, threads are passed in between.

madder

woad

◀ Colours for cloth

Vikings used the leaves, roots, bark and flowers of many plants to dye woollen cloth fabric. For example, a wild flower called weld, or dyer's rocket, produced yellow dye. The roots of the madder plant made a dark red dye. The leaves of woad plants produced a blue dye.

◀ Silken threads

A Japanese craftworker embroiders an intricate design into woven silk using a traditional-style loom. Luxurious and highly decorated textiles were made for the robes of the wealthy. Ordinary people wore plainer clothes of dyed cottons and, occasionally, silk.

porcupine quills

glass beads

▲ Quills and beads

Native Americans have used beads to decorate anything from moccasins to shirts, and to make jewellery. Glass beads brought by traders from the 1500s replaced bone beads and porcupine quills. Quills were usually boiled, dyed and flattened, then woven together to form patterned strips.

◀ Glowing colours

This painting by Diego Rivera shows craftworkers from the region of Tarascan, Central America, dyeing the hanks of yarn before they are woven into cloth. Mesoamerican dyes were made from fruits, flowers, shellfish and the cochineal beetles that lived on cactus plants.

31

Mesoamerican backstrap loom

In South and Central America, homes were not just places to eat and sleep. They were workplaces, too. Weaving was a skill learned by all women in Mesoamerica and in the Andean region, and they spent long hours spinning thread and weaving it into cloth. As well as making tunics, cloaks and other items of clothing for the family, they had to give some to the State as a form of tax payment.

Cotton was spun and woven into textiles for the wealthiest citizens of Mesoamerica. Peasants wore clothes made from the woven fibres of local plants such as the yucca and maguey. Yarn was dyed before it was woven. Most dyes originated from the flowers, fruits and leaves of plants, but some were extracted from shellfish and insects such as the cochineal beetle – a tiny insect that lives on cactus plants.

▲ Skirts, tunics and cloaks
A wealthy Aztec couple sit by the fire, while their hostess cooks a meal. Both of the women are wearing long skirts. The bright embroidery on their tunics is a sign of high rank.

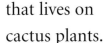

▲ Weaving fibres
Threads spun from plant fibres were woven into cloth on backstrap looms such as this one. Rough fibres from the yucca and cactus plants made coarse cloth. The wealthy had silky textiles.

Down Mexico way ▶
These Mexican women are wearing warm woollen ponchos in bright colours that would also have appealed to their ancestors.

YOU WILL NEED

Two pieces of thick dowelling about 70cm long, brown water-based paint, paintbrush, water pot, string, scissors, thick card, pencil, ruler, masking tape, yellow and red wool, needle.

1 Paint the pieces of dowelling brown. Leave them to dry. Tie a length of string to each length of dowelling and wind it around. Leave a length of string loose at each end.

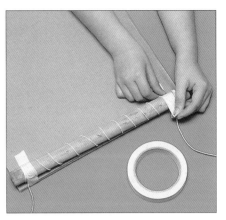

2 Cut a piece of thick card about 100 x 70cm. This is a temporary base. Lightly fix the stringed dowelling at the 70cm sides of the base using masking tape.

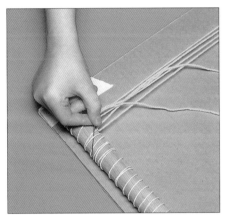

3 Now take your yellow wool. Thread the wool through the string loops using the needle and pull them through to the other end as shown above. Try to keep the yellow wool taut.

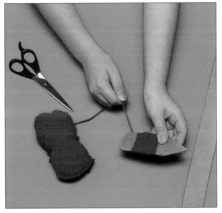

4 Cut a 300 x 35mm piece of thick card. Now cut a smaller rectangle of card with one pointed end as shown above. Wind the red wool tightly around it.

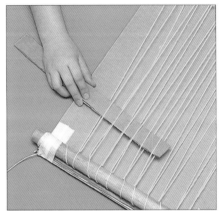

5 Slide the long card rectangle through every second thread. This device, called a shed rod, is turned on its side to lift the threads. Then tie one end of the red wool to the yellow wool.

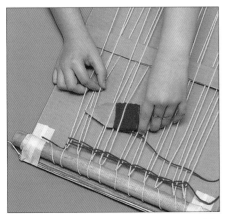

6 Turn the shed rod on its side to lift the threads and feed the red wool through the loom. Then with the shed rod flat, thread the red wool back through alternate yellow threads.

To continue weaving, take the loom off the cardboard base. Tie the loose string around your waist. Attach the other end of the loom to a post or tree with the string. Lean back to keep the long warp threads evenly taut.

Medieval needlework

In medieval Europe, most women were taught to spin and sew. Making small items, such as this medieval-style tapestry design, was a popular pastime. Before any needlework could begin, the canvas background had to be woven, and the yarns spun and dyed. Wool for spinning needlepoint yarn or weaving into cloth came from the sheep on the lord's estate. Linen for fine embroidery and cloth came from flax plants grown in the fields.

Stem stitching

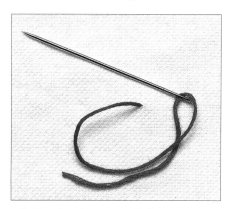

1 Practise the stem stitch on a scrap of old fabric. Push the needle and thread through from the back to the front of the fabric. Hold the end of the thread at the back of the fabric.

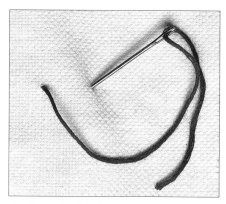

2 Tie a double knot in the thread at the back of the fabric. Then push the needle and thread into the fabric about 5mm along from your first insertion point.

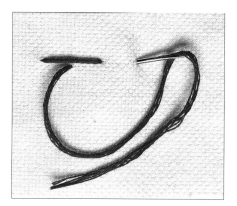

3 Pull the first stitch taut. Bring the needle up just beside the middle of the first stitch. Make a second 5mm stitch. Continue in the same way to make a line.

Medieval needlework

1 Use a black pen to copy the design from step nine on to the tracing paper. Turn the tracing paper over. Trace over the outline you have drawn with the soft-leaded pencil.

2 Tape the tracing paper (pencilled side down) on to the square of fabric. Trace over the motif once again, so that the pencilled image transfers on to the fabric.

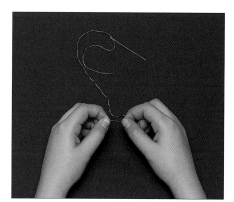

3 Cut a long piece of the orange double-stranded embroidery thread and thread the large-eyed needle. Tie a double knot at one end of the orange thread.

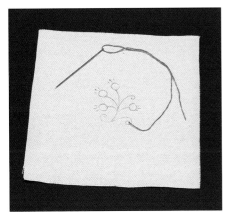

4 Start your embroidery with the scroll shape at the bottom of the design. Push the needle from the back of the fabric to the front. Pull the thread through.

5 Push the thread through the fabric about 2mm along the line of the scroll. Pull the thread through half way along the first stitch. (See Stem stitching on the opposite page.)

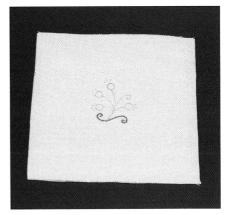

6 Carefully continue your stem stitches all the way along the scroll. The stitches should overlap so that they make a continuous and even, curved line.

7 Thread the needle with a length of green double-stranded embroidery thread. Start at the orange base of the stems and sew along each of the stems in the same way.

8 To sew the flower heads, thread the needle with a length of red embroidery thread. Sew the stem stitch in a circle. Sew a flower head at the end of every stem except one.

9 Thread the needle with the blue embroidery thread. Sew a single stitch for the short details on the flowers and two stitches for the longer, middle ones.

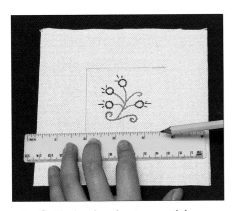

10 Mark a border in pencil 1cm from the edge of the motif. Using a long length of red embroidery thread, follow the pencil lines as a guide for your border stitches.

In medieval times, it was only girls who were taught to sew. Decorative embroidery such as this was mainly done by noblewomen since peasant women could not afford the time or the materials.

American patchwork

The earliest settlers in the USA had to be self-sufficient, because they had little money and the nearest shops were usually in towns far away. They recycled old scraps of material into patchwork designs. Large designs were often stitched on to a linen or cotton backing, with padding in between, to make a quilt. Worn out scraps were transformed into decorative, cosy and long-lasting covers. The women sometimes met up at each other's houses to make quilts. These gatherings were called quilting bees.

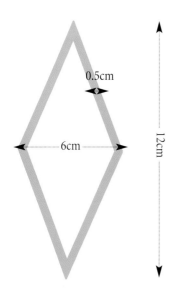

0.5cm

6cm

12cm

1 Copy the diamond-shaped template on to card and cut it out. Draw around the outside edge of the template on to paper. Contine another seven times to form the design shown above.

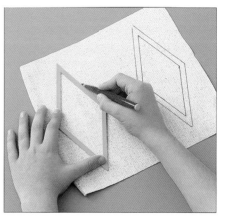

2 Choose six different patterned fabrics of the same thickness. On the back of one of the pieces of fabric, use a felt-tipped pen to draw round the inner and outer edges of the template.

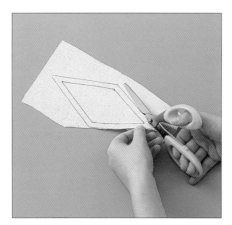

3 Mark out further diamonds on the other pieces of fabric until you have eight altogether. Then cut around the outside edges. The inner line is the edge of the seam – do not cut along it.

4 Arrange the fabric diamonds on the paper design in the way you want them to appear in the final patchwork design. Make sure you are happy with the design before you start to sew.

5 Take two of the diamonds that you want to go next to each other. Place one on top of the other with the patterned sides facing each other. Pin the diamonds together along one edge.

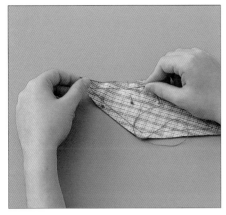

6 Sew the pinned edge of the diamond using a running stitch. Use the inner line that you drew on to the fabric with the template as a guide for the seam.

7 Repeat steps five and six to pin and sew all the diamond fabric pieces together along one of their edges. When you have finished, the fabric pieces will form a star shape.

8 Fold the free edges of the fabric diamonds in along the felt-tipped lines and pin them together. You will be left with a loose corner of fabric at each point of the star.

9 Now use a running stitch to sew down the pinned edges of the fabric diamonds. Try to make the edges as flat and the stitches as small and neat as you can.

10 Turn the star shape over and trim off the loose corners at each point. You should now have a perfect piece of star-shaped patchwork.

11 Pin the star shape carefully in the middle of the blue cushion cover. Then sew it on using small, neat stitches. When you have finished, put a pad in the cushion cover.

Many patchwork designs created by the early settlers became part of the American craft tradition. Patchwork patterns are often given names such as log cabin or nine patch. This one is called eight-pointed star.

Accessories

J ewellery and other decorative accessories have been worn by men and women for thousands of years. Necklaces, earrings, rings, bracelets and ankle rings were made from materials such as shells, feathers, bones, glass beads, gold and precious stones. Accessories can give a clue to the status of the person wearing them. Wealthy people could afford finely crafted ornaments made from rare and expensive materials. Monarchs, priests, warriors and officials often wore badges and other accessories that identified their rank.

▲ Shell necklaces

In ancient times, people wore necklaces made of shells and animal teeth. At this time, jewellery may have been a sign that the wearer was an important person. Necklaces like this one have been found in Asia, as well as Australia. This indicates that the two continents were once linked by a common culture.

pumice stone

ash
face pack

kohl

henna

Cosmetics ▲

In ancient Egypt, black eye kohl was made from galena, a type of poisonous lead. Later on, soot was used. Henna was painted on the nails and the soles of the feet to make them red. Popular beauty treatments included pumice stone to smooth rough skin and ash face packs.

Bead necklaces ▶

Mesopotamian necklaces sometimes had thousands of different beads on several separate strings. The large one here, found at a farming site called Choga Mami, has around 2,200 beads roughly shaped from clay.

Chinese costume ▶

Wealthy Chinese people often wore expensive and well-crafted jewellery, such as gilded pendants made from precious metals and inset with beautiful gemstones. Belt hooks and buckles became an essential part of a Chinese nobleman's clothing from about 300BC. They were highly decorated and made from bronze.

glass

amber

◀ Spiritual headdress

Spiritual leaders called lamas educate people in Buddhism. In Tibet, lamas sometimes wear headdresses for religious services. The one pictured here depicts the five buddhas (enlightened ones) of meditation.

Enamelled brooch ▶

Many of the barbarian invaders of ancient Rome, such as the Visigoths, Vandals and Franks, were skilled craftworkers, as can be seen from this brooch.

◀ Precious amber

Its beautiful shades of gold, yellow and brown made amber extremely popular with Viking jewellers. They also used plain and coloured glass for making fine bead necklaces.

Tribal necklace

Stone Age necklaces were made from all sorts of natural objects, including pebbles, shells, fish bones, animal teeth and claws, nuts and seeds. Later, amber, jade, jet (fossilized coal) and hand-made clay beads were threaded on to thin strips of leather or twine made from plant fibres. Other jewellery included bracelets made of slices of mammoth tusk. People probably decorated their bodies and outlined their eyes with pigments such as red ochre. They may have tattooed and pierced their bodies, too.

YOU WILL NEED

Self-hardening clay, rolling pin, cutting board, modelling tool, sandpaper, ivory and black acrylic paint, paintbrush, water pot, ruler, pencil, 12 x 9cm chamois leather, scissors, card, double-sided sticky tape, PVA glue and glue brush, leather laces.

1 Roll out the clay on to a board. Cut out three crescent shapes with the modelling tool. Leave to dry. Rub the crescents gently with sandpaper and paint them an ivory colour.

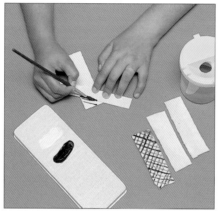

2 Cut four strips of leather to measure 9 x 3cm. Use the edge of a piece of card as a guide for your brush and make a criss-cross pattern on the strips of leather as shown.

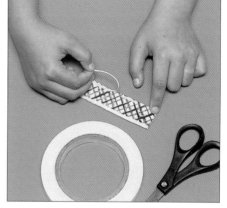

3 When the strips of leather are completely dry, fold the side edges of each strip in. Stick them securely in place with a piece of double-sided sticky tape.

4 Brush glue on the middle of each clay crescent. Wrap a strip of leather around a crescent, leaving enough to form a loop at the top. Glue the loops in place. Paint three lines on each loop.

5 Plait three leather laces to make a thong to fit around your neck. Thread on the leopard's claws. Arrange the claws so that there are small spaces between them.

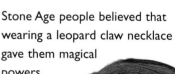

Stone Age people believed that wearing a leopard claw necklace gave them magical powers.

Egyptian mirror

The ancient Egyptians were fond of cosmetics. Cleopatra, who ruled Egypt in 51BC, used one of the first moisturisers to protect her skin from the effects of the desert sand. Both men and women wore green eyeshadow made from a mineral called malachite and black eyeliner made from a type of lead called galena. Mirrors were used by wealthy Egyptians for checking hairstyles, applying make-up or simply admiring their looks. The mirrors were made of polished copper or bronze, with handles of wood or ivory.

YOU WILL NEED

Self-hardening clay, modelling tool, cutting board, small piece of card or sandpaper, wire baking tray, small plate, mirror card, pencil, scissors, gold paint, paintbrush, water pot, PVA glue and glue brush.

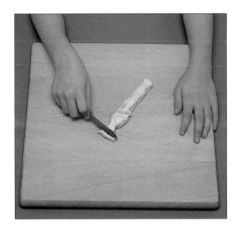

1 Roll a piece of self-hardening clay into a tube. Mould the tube into a handle shape. Use the modelling tool to decorate the handle in the shape of a god or with a flower design.

2 Make a slot in the handle with a piece of card or sandpaper. Place the handle on a wire baking tray and leave it in a warm place to dry. Turn the handle over after two hours.

3 Draw round a small plate on to the mirror card. Add a pointed bit to fit in the slot in the handle. Cut the mirror shape out. When the handle is dry, insert the mirror in the slot.

4 It is now time to paint the handle. Paint one side carefully with gold paint and leave it to dry. When it has dried, turn the handle over and paint the other side.

5 Finally, you can assemble your mirror. Cover the base of the mirror card in glue and insert it into the handle slot. Now your mirror is ready to use.

The shiny surfaces and shapes of mirrors reminded Egyptians of the sun's disc, so they became religious symbols.

Egyptian pectoral

Archaeologists know that the Egyptians loved jewellery, because so much has been unearthed in their tombs. Some are beautifully made from precious stones and costly metals. Other pieces are much simpler and are made from materials such as pottery and bone. The Egyptian original of this pectoral (necklace) was made by a technique called *cloisonné*. Gold wire was worked into a framework with lots of little compartments or *cloisons*. These were filled with coloured enamel (glass) paste. Then the piece was fired.

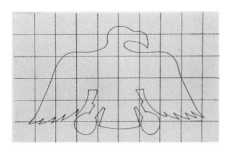

1 Take a sheet of A4 paper and draw vertical lines 2cm apart and then horizontal lines 2cm apart to make a grid as shown. Copy the design above on to the grid, one square at a time.

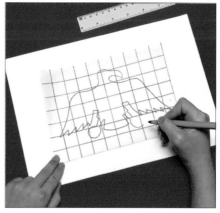

2 Place the tracing paper over the design. Use masking tape to secure it. Use a pen and ruler to trace your design and the grid on to the tracing paper. Cut out the falcon shape.

3 Place the self-hardening clay on to a cutting board. Use a rolling pin to flatten it out. Roll out the clay to measure 21 x 15cm in size with a thickness of 5cm.

4 Use masking tape to fix the tracing paper to the clay. Trace the design and then use the modelling tool to cut around the outline of the falcon. Make sure you cut right through the clay.

5 Remove the tracing paper. Use a fine modelling tool to mould the detail. Use a cocktail stick to make a 3mm hole on each wing, 2cm away from the top edge of the wing.

6 Leave the clay falcon to dry in a warm room. Use a medium-sized paintbrush and blue acrylic paint to colour body and wings of the falcon. Leave it to dry completely.

7 Use red, blue, green and gold acrylic paints to add decorative touches to the falcon as shown above. Try to make the design look as if it is really made of precious gems and gold.

8 Clean the paintbrush in water and leave the falcon to dry. Use the clean brush to apply a thin coat of wood varnish over the model. Then clean the paintbrush with white spirit.

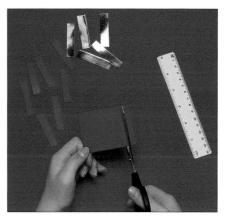

9 Paint five 5cm square pieces of plain paper blue and five pieces gold. Cut each square into strips, each 1cm wide. You will need 25 strips of each colour in total.

10 When the strips are dry, roll each one around a pen. Dab PVA glue on to the ends of the paper to stick them. Use masking tape to secure the ends of the paper until dry.

11 When the glue is dry, remove the tape and paint the paper tubes with red, blue and gold dots as shown above. You now have 50 beads to make a necklace.

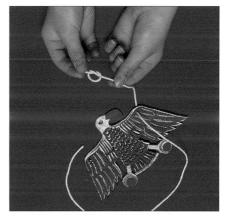

12 Cut two lengths of string, each 45cm long. Thread one end of each piece of string through the holes in the falcon's wings. Tie a knot in the strings.

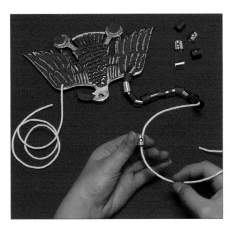

13 Thread the beads on to the pieces of string. Alternate the blue and gold beads. You should thread 25 beads on to each string to make the decorative necklace.

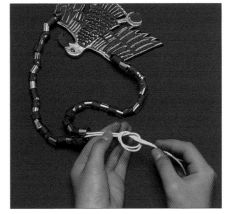

14 Finish threading all the beads on to the string. Tie the ends of the two pieces of string with a secure knot. Trim off excess string to finish off your necklace.

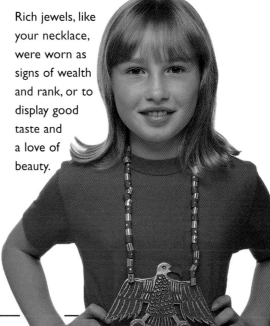

Rich jewels, like your necklace, were worn as signs of wealth and rank, or to display good taste and a love of beauty.

Chinese fan

Court dress in China varied greatly over the ages. Foreign invasions brought new fashions and dress codes. Government officials wore elegant robes that reflected their rank and social status. Beautiful silk robes patterned with *lung pao* (dragons) were worn by court ladies, officials and the emperor himself. Many people, both men and women, might carry a fan as a symbol of good upbringing as well as to provide a cool breeze in the sweltering summer heat.

fan

YOU WILL NEED

Red tissue paper, thick card base (40 x 20cm), masking tape, pair of compasses, ruler, pencil, acrylic paints (pink, light blue, cream, light green), paintbrush, water pot, scissors, 16 x 1cm balsa strips (x15), barbecue stick, PVA glue and glue brush, thin card.

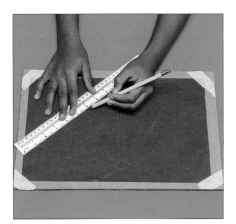

1 Tape tissue paper on to the base. Draw two semicircles (16cm radius and 7cm radius) from one side of the base. Then draw even lines about 1cm apart between the two semicircles.

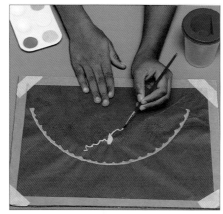

2 Draw a design on to the tissue paper. Paint in the details and leave the paint to dry. Then remove the paper from the base and cut out the fan along edges of the semicircles.

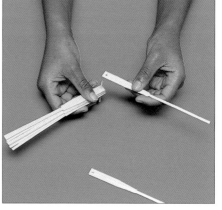

3 Use scissors to cut a slither off each side of each balsa strip for half its length. Pierce a compass hole at the wide base of the strip. Thread the strips on to a barbecue stick.

4 Fold the decorated tissue paper backwards and forwards to form a concertina. Glue each alternate fold of the paper to the narrow ends of the balsa strips as shown above.

5 Paint the outer strips of the fan pink and let the paint dry. Cut out two small card discs. Glue them over the ends of the barbecue stick to secure the strips as shown above.

The earliest Chinese fans were made of feathers or of silk stretched over a flat frame. The folding fan came later.

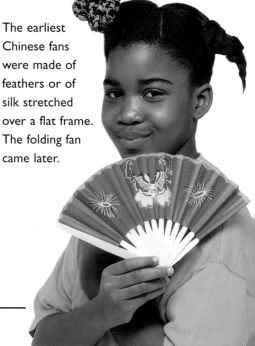

Japanese fan

Until 1500, Japanese court fashions were based on traditional Chinese styles. Men and women wore long, flowing robes made of many layers of fine, glossy silk, held in place by a sash and cords. Flat fans, or *uchiwa*, like the one in this project, could be tucked into the sash when not in use. In the 1500s, *kimonos* (long, loose robes) became popular among wealthy artists, actors and craftworkers. Women wore wide silk sashes called *obis* on top of their kimonos. Men fastened their kimonos with narrow sashes.

YOU WILL NEED

Thick card measuring 38 x 26cm, pencil, ruler, pair of compasses, protractor, blue felt tip pen, red paper measuring 30 x 26cm, scissors, acrylic paints, paintbrush, water pot, glue stick.

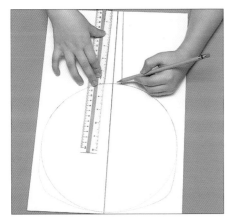

1 Draw a line down the centre of the piece of thick card. Draw a circle 23cm wide two-thirds of the way up. Add squared-off edges at the top of the circle. Draw a 15cm long handle.

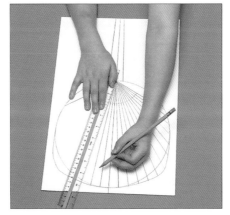

2 Place a protractor at the top of the handle and draw a semicircle around it. Now mark lines every 2.5 degrees. Draw pencil lines through these marks to the edge of the circle.

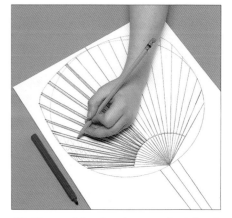

3 Draw a blue line 1cm to the left of each pencil mark. Then draw a blue line 2mm to the right of each of the pencil marks. Pencil in a rough squiggle in between the blue sections.

4 Cut out the fan. Draw around the fan shape on the red paper. Cut it out. Leave to one side. Then cut out the sections marked with squiggles on the white fan. Paint the white fan brown.

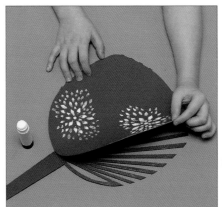

5 Leave the fan to dry. Paint the red paper with white flowers and leave to dry. Paste glue on to one side of the card fan. Stick the undecorated side of the red card to the fan.

Japanese noble ladies hid their faces in court. They used decorated fans such as this one as a screen.

Japanese netsuke fox

There is a long tradition among Japanese craftworkers of making everyday things as beautiful as possible. Craftworkers also created exquisite items for the wealthiest and most knowledgeable collectors. They used a wide variety of materials, including pottery, metal, lacquer, cloth, paper and bamboo. Ceramics ranged from plain, simple earthenware to delicate porcelain painted with brilliantly coloured glazes. Japanese metalworkers produced alloys (mixtures of metals) that were unknown elsewhere in the ancient world. Cloth was woven from many fibres in elaborate designs. Bamboo and other grasses were woven into elegant *tatami* (floor mats) and containers of all different shapes and sizes. Japanese craftworkers also made beautiful *inro*. These are little boxes, used like purses, that dangled from men's kimono sashes using a *netsuke* (carved toggle).

▲ **Keeping it safe**
Carved ivory or wooden toggles, called netsuke, were used to hold the inro in the waist sash of a kimono. Netsuke were shaped into representations of gods, dragons or living animals.

▲ **Boxes for belts**
These small boxes were originally designed for storing medicines. The first inro were plain and simple, but after about 1700 they were often decorated with exquisite designs. These inro have been lacquered (coated with a shiny substance made from the sap of the lacquer tree). Inside, they contain several compartments stacked on top of each other.

YOU WILL NEED

Paper, pencil, ruler, rolling pin, self-hardening clay, cutting board, modelling tool, balsa wood, fine sandpaper, acrylic paint, paintbrush water pot, darning needle, cord, small box (for an inro), scissors, toggle, wide belt.

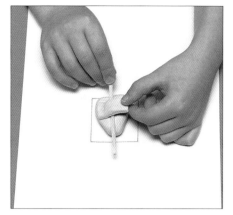

1 Draw a 5 x 5cm square on to the paper. Roll out some clay to the size of the square. Shape a point at one end. Lay a small length of balsa along the back. Secure it with a thin strip of clay.

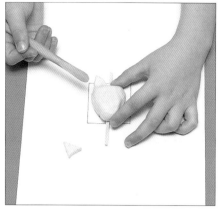

2 Turn the clay back on its right side. Cut out two triangles of clay for the ears. Join them to the head using a modelling tool. Make indentations to shape them into the ears of a fox.

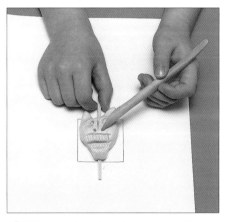

3 Use the handle of your modelling tool to make the fox's mouth. Carve eyes, nostrils, teeth and a frown line. Use the blunt end of the pencil to make holes for the fox's eyes.

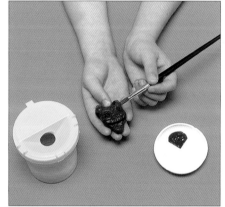
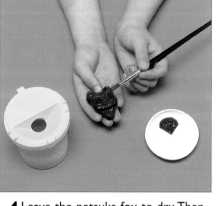

4 Leave the netsuke fox to dry. Then gently sand the netsuke and remove the balsa wood stick. Paint the netsuke with several layers of acrylic paint. Leave it in a warm place to dry.

Wear your inro dangling from your belt. In ancient Japan inro were usually worn by men. They were held in place by carved toggles called netsuke.

5 Thread some cord through four corners of a small box with a darning needle. Then thread the cord through the toggle and the hole on the netsuke left by the balsa wood.

6 Put a wide belt round your waist. Thread the netsuke under the belt. It should rest on the top of the belt as shown above. The inro (box) should hang down.

Native American anklets

Most of the wars between different Native American tribes were fought over land or hunting territory, and later over horses. As European settlers began to occupy more land, many tribes fought to stop them. Before going into battle, Native American warriors performed a war dance to ask for spiritual guidance and protection during the conflict. Ceremonial dress and body painting was a feature of these occasions. The anklets in this project are similar to the ones worn by many tribes during their war dances.

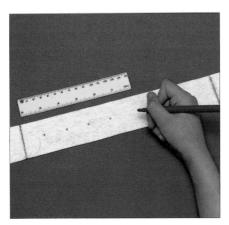

1 Mark two lines across the felt strips, 24cm in from each end. Make a series of marks in between these lines. Start 3cm away from the line, then mark at 3cm intervals.

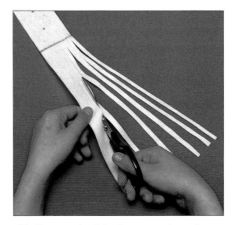

2 Create the fringing at each end of the anklet. Do this by cutting into both ends of the band up to the marked lines. Repeat the process for the other anklet.

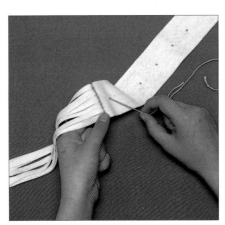

3 Thread a large needle with strong, doubled and knotted thread. Insert the needle into the fabric and pull through until the knot hits the fabric.

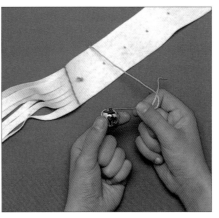

4 Thread a bell over the needle and up to the felt. Push the needle back through the felt. Knot the end on the opposite side to the bell. Trim excess thread. Repeat for the other seven bells.

Tie the anklets round your ankles. The bells of the North American Indians were sewn on to strips of animal hide. They were tied around the ankles and just under the knees and worn for ceremonial dances.

Native American necklace

Tribes in North America took pride in their appearance. As well as wearing decorative necklaces, headdresses and other jewellery, many tribes wore tattoos as a sign of status or to gain protection from spirits. Hairstyles were important, too, and could indicate that a young man was unmarried or belonged to a warrior class. Woodlands men had a distinctive hairstyle. They braided their hair at the front and decorated it with turkey feathers. Some Plains warriors shaved their heads completely, leaving a long tuft on top.

YOU WILL NEED

Thin white paper strips, PVA glue and glue brush, acrylic paints (blue, turquoise and red), paintbrush, water pot, scissors, self-hardening clay, skewer, string.

1 Roll up the strips of thin white paper into 5mm tubes. Glue down the outer edge to seal the tubes and leave them to dry. Make three of these paper tubes.

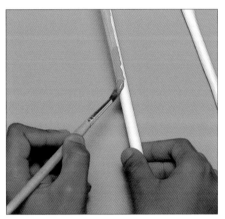

2 When the glue has dried, paint the rolls of paper. Paint one roll blue, one roll red and one roll turquoise, making sure that you cover all the white areas. Leave them to dry.

3 When they have dried, the painted paper tubes will have hardened slightly. Carefully cut the tubes to separate them into 1cm pieces. These will be the beads of your necklace.

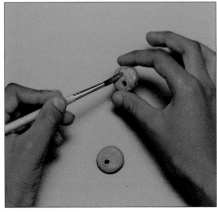

4 Roll the clay into two large clay beads. Pierce the centres with a skewer. Leave the beads to dry and harden. When they are ready, paint both of the beads blue. Leave to dry.

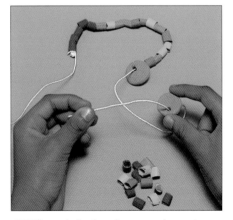

5 Thread the beads on to the string. Start with the clay beads which will hang in the centre. Then add blue either side, then turquoise, then red. Knot the ends together when you have finished.

Native Americans made beads from bone, stone and shell. Some of their bone beads were 8–10cm long. European traders introduced glass beads in the 1500s.

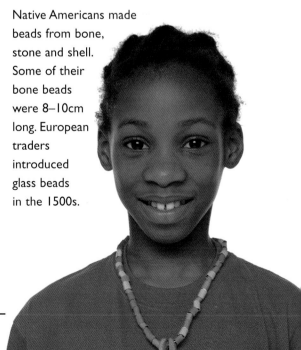

Glass bead jewellery

Native Americans were not only hunters and warriors, they were also artists and craftworkers. Tribespeople made everything they needed for themselves, from clothes and blankets to tools and weapons. The first settlers from Europe took coloured glass beads with them to the USA. Many Native American tribes bargained with traders for the beads. They developed great skill in using them to make brilliant, richly coloured patterns on dresses, trousers, shoes and many other possessions.

YOU WILL NEED

70cm piece of narrow leather thong, ruler, scissors, 165cm strong waxed thread, selection of glass and silver beads in different sizes, four brightly coloured dyed feathers, two glass and two silver beads with holes big enough to cover the knotted leather thong.

1 To make a Native American glass bead necklace, cut two strips of leather thong, each 15cm long. You will use these strips to tie the finished necklace around your neck.

2 Next, take the waxed thread and carefully cut off one long piece about 25cm long using the scissors. Then cut four smaller pieces of waxed thread, each 10cm long.

3 Knot one end of one leather strip to one end of the 25cm-long waxed thread. Thread on one of the glass or silver beads with a hole that will cover the knot you have made.

4 Thread different beads on to the long piece of waxed thread until there is about a 10cm gap left at the end. Thread the beads in a repeating pattern or randomly, as you prefer.

5 Now make the four dangling pieces of the necklace. For each one, tie one end of the 10cm-long piece of waxed thread around the quill of a brightly coloured feather.

6 Thread on some smaller beads, covering only half of each piece of waxed thread. Tie a knot to secure the beads. Again, you can thread them in a pattern if you like.

7 Tie each feathery piece on to the main necklace. Then tie on the second 15cm-long leather thong at the free end. Cover the knot with one of the glass or silver beads with a big hole.

8 To make a bracelet to match your necklace, cut two 20cm long strips of leather thong. When the bracelet is finished, you will use these to tie it around your wrist.

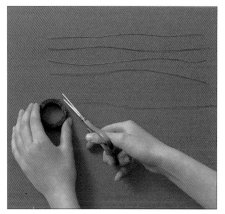

9 Next, cut five lengths of waxed thread, each measuring about 20cm in length. These threads are going to form the main part of your beaded bracelet.

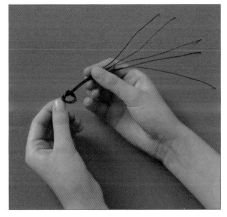

10 Take the five lengths of waxed thread, and tie a big knot at one end to join them all together. Try to make the knot as small and as neat as possible.

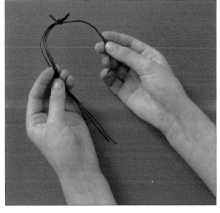

11 Take the knotted end of the waxed threads and carefully tie on one of the leather strips. Cover the knot with one of the glass or silver beads with a big hole.

Jewellery like this is still sold in the western USA. Today, Native Americans make all sorts of different jewellery items for the tourist trade.

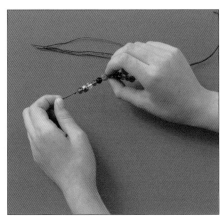

12 Thread some beads on to one of the waxed threads, keeping some thread spare. You can make a pattern or not, as you prefer. Then tie a knot to keep the beads in place.

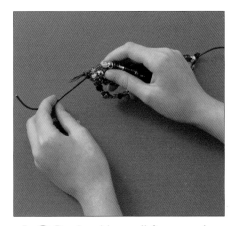

13 Bead and knot all five waxed threads and then tie them all together. Tie on the last leather strip and cover the knot with a large bead. Now your bracelet is ready to wear.

Arctic purse

Surviving in the Arctic was hard. Men and women had to work long hours to keep everyone warm, clothed and fed. Women looked after the domestic chores. Their work included tending the fire, cooking, preparing animal hides and looking after their children. Arctic women were also skilled at craftwork, and sewing was an extremely important job. They had to find time to make and repair all the family's clothes and bedding, as well as make items such as bags, purses and other useful containers.

> ## YOU WILL NEED
>
> Chamois leather (21 x 35cm), PVA glue and glue brush, pencil, ruler, scissors, shoelace (50cm long), pieces of decorative felt (red, dark blue and light blue), two blue beads.

1 Fold the chamois leather in half. Glue down two sides, leaving one end open. Pencil in marks 1cm apart on either side of the open end. Make small holes at these points with the scissors.

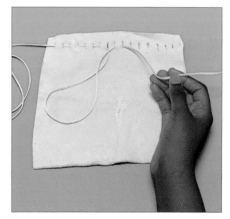

2 Thread a shoelace through the holes on both sides as shown above. Tie the ends of the shoelace together and leave an excess piece of lace hanging.

3 Carefully cut two strips of red felt 21cm long and 5cm wide. Then mark and cut a narrow fringe about 1cm deep along both edges of each red felt piece as shown.

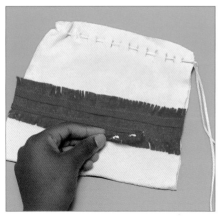

4 Glue strips of red fringing felt to either side of the purse. Add extra decoration by sticking 1cm strips of dark blue and light blue felt on top of the red fringing felt and the purse.

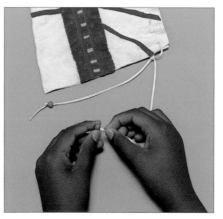

5 Tie the two blue beads securely to each of the excess shoelace. Close the purse by pulling the shoelace and tying a knot in it. Your Arctic purse is ready to use.

Drawstring purses such as this one were often made of soft deer hide called buckskin.

Celtic mirror

Metalworkers made many valuable Celtic items, from iron swords to the beautiful bronze handles of their mirrors. Patterns and techniques invented in one part of the Celtic world quickly spread to others. Metalworkers excelled in several different techniques. Heavy objects were cast from solid bronze using a clay mould. Thin sheets of silver and bronze were decorated with *repoussé* (pushed out) designs. The designs were sketched on to the back of the metal, then gently hammered to create raised patterns.

YOU WILL NEED

Pair of compasses, pencil, ruler, stiff gold mirror card, scissors, tracing paper, pen, self-hardening clay, cutting board, gold paint, paintbrush, water pot, PVA glue and glue brush.

1 Use the compasses to draw a circle with a diameter of 22cm on to the gold card. Cut the gold circle out. Use this circle as a template to draw a second circle on to gold card.

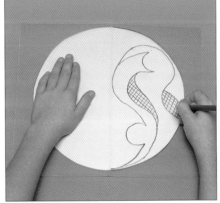

2 Cut out the second gold circle. Draw another circle on to some tracing paper. Fold the piece of tracing paper in half and draw on a Celtic pattern like the one shown above.

3 Lay the tracing paper on to one of the circles. Trace the pattern on to half of the gold circle, then turn the paper over and repeat the tracing. Go over the pattern with a pen.

4 Roll out several pieces of clay and sculpt them into a handle about 15cm long and 9cm wide. Leave to dry. Paint one side with gold paint. Leave to dry. Turn over and paint the other side.

5 Stick the two pieces of mirror card together, white side to white side, with the gold sides facing out as shown above. Glue the handle on to the side of the mirror when the paint has dried.

The bronze on a Celtic mirror would have been polished so that the owner could see his or her reflection on it.

Celtic torc

The Celts were skilled at many different crafts, including glass, jewellery, enamel and metalwork. Only wealthy people could afford items made from gold. Celtic chiefs often rewarded their best warriors with rich gifts of fine gold armbands. Heavy necklaces called torcs were also highly prized. The Celts believed that torcs had the power to protect people from evil spirits. For the same reason, the Celts often painted or tattooed their bodies with a dark blue dye taken from a plant called woad.

YOU WILL NEED

Self-hardening clay, cutting board, ruler, string, scissors, PVA glue and glue brush, gold or bronze paint, paintbrush, water pot.

1 Roll out two lengths of clay about 60cm long and about 1cm thick on the cutting board. Twist the rolls together, leaving about 5cm of untwisted clay at either end.

2 Make loops out of the untwisted ends of the clay torc by joining them together as shown above. Dampen the ends with a little water to help join the clay if necessary.

3 Use a ruler to measure an opening between the two looped ends. The ends should be about 9cm apart so that the torc will fit easily around your neck. Let the torc begin to dry.

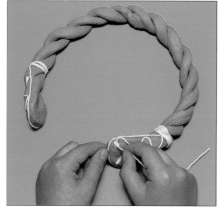

4 When the torc is partially dry, cut two pieces of string about 8cm in length. Use the string to decorate the looped ends of the torc. Glue the string securely in place.

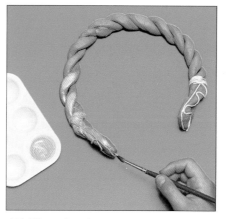

5 Allow the clay torc to dry out completely. When it is hard, cover the torc and decorative string with gold or bronze paint. Leave to dry again before you wear your torc.

Celtic torcs were made from precious metals such as iron, bronze and gold.

Celtic brooch

Looking good was important to Celtic men and women because it made people admire them. Ancient Roman reports suggest that different groups of men within Celtic society cut their hair and shaved their faces in different styles to show their status. Legends told that warriors who did not have naturally blonde hair (preferred by the Celts) bleached it with a mixture of urine and wood-ash. Jewellery was extremely important to the Celts. Bracelets, brooches and torcs were worn by all members of Celtic society.

YOU WILL NEED

Self-hardening clay, rolling pin, cutting board, modelling tool, sharp pencil, sandpaper, acrylic paints (light blue, dark blue and white), paintbrush, water pot, large safety pin, sticky tape.

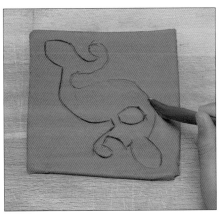

1 Roll out a 15 x 15cm square of clay on to the cutting board. It should be about 5mm thick. Copy a dragon shape on to the clay, using the finished brooch as a guide.

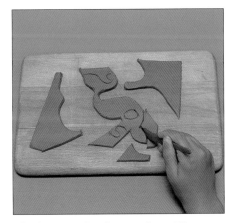

2 Cut out the dragon shape. Then use the modelling tool to draw some of the features of the dragon into the centre of your brooch as shown above.

3 Cut the centre hole out of the brooch. Add the dragon's two faces and more patterns using a modelling tool. Finish the patterns with the sharp end of a pencil. Let the brooch dry.

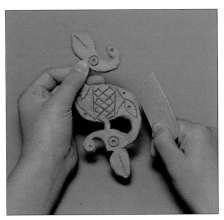

4 When the brooch has dried, gently hold it in one hand. With your other hand, sand the edges with a piece of smooth sandpaper until they are completely smooth.

5 Paint the brooch light blue. Add dark blue and white decoration as shown above. Let the brooch dry. Stick a large safety pin on the back of the brooch with sticky tape.

The brooch that inspired this design was called a dragon brooch. It was made in Britain in around AD100.

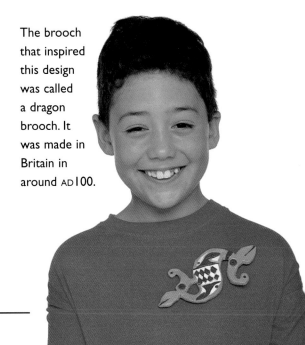

Viking brooches

The Vikings loved showy jewellery, especially armbands, rings and gold and silver necklaces. These were often decorated with ornate designs. Jewellery was a sign of wealth and could be used instead of money to buy other goods.

Brooches were worn by Viking women. Typical dress for Viking women and girls was a long plain shift. It was made of wool or linen. Over this they wore a woollen tunic, with shoulder straps secured by ornate brooches. Between the brooches there was often a chain or a string of beads.

YOU WILL NEED

Self-hardening clay, rolling board, ruler, string, scissors, PVA glue and brush, bronze paint, A4 sheet of white paper, water pot, paintbrush, pair of compasses, pencil, tracing paper, gold foil, card, safety pin.

1 Roll two balls of clay into slightly domed disc shapes 2-3cm across. Let them dry. Glue string borders around them. Paint them with bronze paint. Leave them to dry.

2 Use compasses to draw two circles on a sheet of white paper. Make them the same size as your brooch shapes. Draw a Viking pattern in your circle or copy the one shown above.

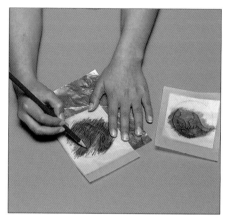

3 Use tracing paper to trace each pattern on to a piece of gold foil. Cut the patterns out in small pieces that will interlink. Take care not to tear the foil.

4 Glue each piece of the foil pattern on to the outside of one of the clay brooches. Leave the brooch to dry. Then glue the foil pattern on to the other clay brooch.

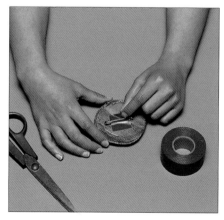

5 Cut and stick a circle of painted gold card on to the back of each brooch. Fix a safety pin on to the back of each brooch with masking tape. Your brooches are now ready to wear.

Brooches were important pieces of jewellery. They were used as fasteners for cloaks and tunics.

Viking bracelet

All Vikings turned their hand to craftwork. Men carved ivory and wood during the long winter evenings, and women made woollen cloth. Professional craftworkers worked gold, silver and bronze and made fine jewellery from gemstones, amber and jet. Other beautiful objects were carved from antlers or walrus tusks. Homes and churches had beautiful wood carvings. Patterns included swirling loops and knots, and birds and animals interlaced with writhing snakes and strange monsters.

YOU WILL NEED

Tape measure, self-hardening clay, cutting board, white cord or string, scissors, modelling tool, silver paint, paintbrush, water pot.

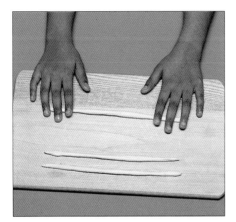

1 Measure your wrist with a tape measure. Roll three clay snakes just longer than the size of your wrist. This will ensure that the bracelet will pass over your hand but not fall off.

2 Lay out the clay snakes in a fan shape. Then cut two lengths of white cord a bit longer than the snakes, and plait the clay snakes and the two cords together as shown above.

3 Trim each end of the clay and cord plait with a modelling tool. At each end, press the strands firmly together and secure them with a small roll of clay as shown above.

4 Carefully curl the bracelet round so it will fit neatly around your wrist. Make sure you leave the ends open. Leave the bracelet in a safe place to dry thoroughly.

5 When the bracelet is completely dry, paint it with silver paint. Give it a second coat if necessary. Leave the bracelet to dry again. When it is completely dry you can try it on.

Vikings liked to show off their rank by wearing expensive gold and silver jewellery.

Aztec feather fan

Countless tropical birds live in Central America. Their brightly coloured feathers became an important item of trade in the Aztec world. Birds were hunted and raised in captivity for their feathers, which were arranged into elaborate patterns and designs. Skilled Aztec featherworkers wove beautiful garments, such as decorative headdresses, feather *ponchos* (shirts) and fans. Jewellery was popular, too, but it could only be worn by the ruler and the nobility. Earrings, necklaces, labrets (lip-plugs) and bracelets made of gold and precious stones were all popular items. As well as wearing jewellery, tattooing was a widespread practice in Mesoamerica.

▲ Tax collection
The Aztecs loved feather decoration. These pictures show items that were collected as a form of tax payment from the lands they conquered.

◀ Feather work
The Aztecs had an expert guild of featherworkers who used complicated methods of gluing and weaving to make items such as headdresses and fans.

YOU WILL NEED

Pair of compasses, pencil, ruler, thick card (90 x 45cm), scissors, thin red card, green paper, double-sided sticky tape, feathers (real or paper), roll of masking tape, acrylic paints, paintbrushes, water pot, coloured felt, PVA glue and glue brush, single-sided sticky tape, coloured wool, bamboo cane.

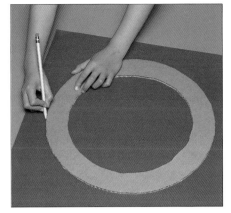

1 Use the compasses to draw two rings about 45cm in diameter and 8cm wide on thick card. Cut them out. Use a thick card ring to make another ring from the thin red card as above.

2 Cut lots of leaf shapes from green paper. Stick them around the edge of one thick card ring using double-sided sticky tape. Add some real feathers or ones made from paper.

3 Cut two circles about 12cm in diameter from thin red card. Draw around something the right size, such as a roll of masking tape. These circles will be the centre of your feather fan.

4 Paint a flower on to one of the two smaller red circles and a butterfly on the other. Cut lots of v-shapes from the felt and glue them to the large red ring.

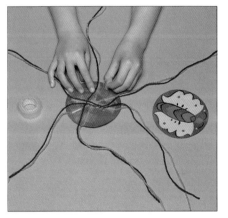

5 Using single-sided sticky tape, fix lengths of coloured wool to the back of one of the red circles as shown above. Place this red circle in the centre of the leafy ring.

6 Tape the wool to the outer ring. Glue the second card ring on top. Insert the cane in between. Stick the second red circle face up in the centre. Glue the larger, outer ring on top.

Aztec nobles and rulers were cooled with beautiful feather fans such as the one you have made.

Buckles and badges

In the Wild West, lawmen wore a metal star pinned on the front of their jackets to identify themselves. It was their job to keep law and order. The first project here shows you how to make your own sheriff's badge.

Every belt needs a buckle, and one way a cowboy could get a new one was to win it as a prize at a special contest called a rodeo. Wearing this would show his friends how skilful he was as a cowboy. The second part of this project shows you how to make a prize belt buckle of your own.

▲ **Tools of the trade**
Cowboys had tough lives and wore tough, practical clothes. This cowboy wears a gun at his belt and carries a rope lasso, or lariat, for roping cattle.

YOU WILL NEED

Self-hardening clay, rolling pin, cutting board, ruler, star-shaped pastry cutter, PVA glue and glue brush, kebab stick or sharpened pencil, water, flowerpot, modelling tool, large safety pin with flat plate, two strips of bias binding tape, 8cm long needle and thread, silver poster paint, paintbrush, water pot, permanent black marker.

1 Roll a handful of clay out into two circles, each 5mm thick. With the star-shaped pastry cutter, press out a star from one of the clay circles. Lift the star from the surrounding clay.

2 Roll out some of the excess clay to make six tiny balls. Each one should be about half the size of your fingernail. Glue each ball on a point of the star shape.

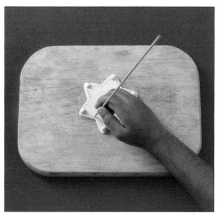

3 Use the pointed end of a kebab stick or a sharpened pencil to make a line of tiny dots around the edge of the star shape. Try to be as neat as you possibly can.

4 To give the star a curved shape, lightly brush the back of the star with water and press it on to the side of a flowerpot. Peel the star away gently. Leave it to dry overnight.

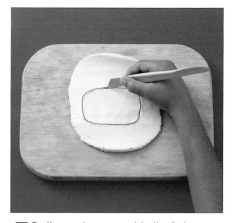

5 Roll out the second ball of clay. Use a modelling tool to cut a rectangular shape with rounded corners as shown. The rectangle should measure about 8 x 5cm.

6 Follow step 2 again to make 12 more tiny modelling clay balls with excess clay. Then carefully glue the balls around the edge of the clay buckle.

7 Once again, use the pointed end of a kebab stick or a sharpened pencil to add some decorative touches to the parts of the buckle between the balls with dots and swirls.

8 Follow step 4 again to give the buckle a curved shape. When you are happy with the shape of the buckle, peel it off gently. Then leave it to dry overnight.

9 After 24 hours, when the clay star badge is dry, glue the plate of the safety pin to the back of the star. Carefully attach the pin to the flat space in the middle of the badge.

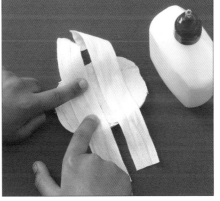

10 When the buckle is completely dry, glue two strips of bias binding tape across the back of the buckle. Use a running stitch to sew the ends together to make two loops.

Thread a thick leather belt through the loops on the back of your buckle and pin on your sheriff's badge – you are ready to hunt down those outlaws!

11 When the glue on the badge and buckle is completely dry, you can paint them both with silver paint to give them an authentic metallic sheen.

12 When the paint has dried, you can add the finishing touches using a permanent black marker. Try drawing a star shape in the middle of the badge and the buckle.

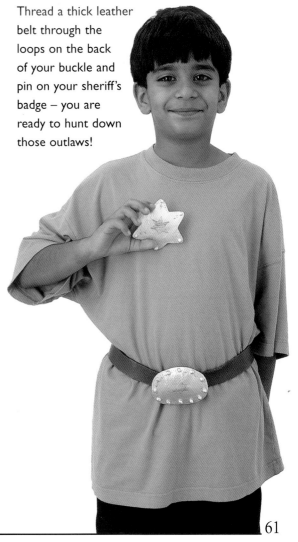

Glossary

A

aristocracy A ruling class of wealthy, privileged people, or government by such people.

armour A suit or covering worn by people or horses to protect them against injury during battle.

artefact An object that has been preserved from the past.

Aztec Mesoamerican people who lived in northern and central Mexico. The Aztecs were most powerful between 1350 and 1520.

B

Before Christ (BC) A system used to calculate dates before the supposed year of Jesus Christ's birth. Dates are calculated in reverse. For example, 2000BC is longer ago than 200BC.

brahmin A Hindu who belongs to the highest of four social classes.

Bronze Age A period in human history, between 3000 and 1000BC, when tools and weapons were made from bronze.

Buddhism World religion founded in ancient India by the Buddha in the 6th century BC.

C

caste One of four social classes that divide the followers of Hinduism.

Celt A member of one of the ancient peoples that inhabited most parts of Europe from around 750BC to AD1000.

century A period of 100 years. Also a unit of the Roman army, numbering up to 100 foot soldiers.

ceramics The art and technique of making pottery.

chainmail Flexible armour for the body, consisting of small rings of metal, linked to form a fine mesh.

chaps Over-trousers worn by cowboys to protect their legs.

chiton Long tunics worn by both men and women in ancient Greece. Chitons were draped loosely over the body and held in place with brooches or pins.

circa (*c.*) A symbol used to mean 'approximately,' when the exact date of an event is not known e.g. *c.*1000BC.

civilization A society that makes advances in arts, sciences, law, technology and government.

cuirass Armour that protects the upper part of the body.

G

geisha A Japanese woman who entertains men with song and dances.

gem A precious or semi-precious stone or crystal, such as diamond or ruby. Gems often decorate jewellery or other ornaments.

glyph A picture symbol used in writing.

government A body of people, usually elected, with the power to control the affairs of a country or state.

greaves Armour worn to protect the shins.

I

inro A small, decorated box that is worn hanging from the sash of a Japanese kimono.

inscribed Lettering, pictures or patterns carved into a hard material such as stone or wood.

Inuit The native people of the Arctic regions of Greenland, Alaska and Canada.

Iron Age The period when iron became the main metal used for producing tools and weapons. The Iron Age began around 1200BC.

iron ore Rock that contains iron in a raw, natural form.

Islam A world religion founded in the 7th century AD by the prophet Mohammed.

K

kanji The picture symbols based on Chinese characters that were used for writing Japanese before about AD800.

kimono A loose wide-sleeved robe, worn by both men and women in Japan.

L

loom A frame used for weaving cloth.

M

Maya An ancient civilization native to Mesamerica.

Medieval A term describing people, events and objects from a period in history known as the Middle Ages.

Mesoamerica A geographical area made up of the land between Mexico and Panama in Central America.

Mesopotamia An ancient name for the fertile region between the Tigris and Euphrates rivers in the Middle East. This area is now occupied by Iraq.

Middle Ages Period in history that lasted from around AD800 to 1400.

N

Native Americans The indigenous peoples of the Americas.

neolithic The New Stone Age. The period when people began to farm but were still using stone tools.

netsuke Small Japanese toggles that are carved from ivory and used to secure items from the sash of a kimono.

P

plate armour Protective clothing made of overlapping plates of solid metal.

prehistoric The period in history before written records were made.

S

Sari A traditional garment worn by Indian women. A sari consists of a long piece of fabric wound round the waist and draped over one shoulder and sometimes the head.

shield boss A metal plate that is fixed to the centre of a shield to protect the hand of the person holding it.

spindle A rod used to twist fibres into yarn for weaving.

Stone Age The first period in human history, in which people made their tools and weapons out of stone.

surcoat A long, loose tunic worn over body armour.

T

tax Goods, money or services paid to the government or ruling state.

textile Cloth produced by weaving threads, such as silk or cotton, together.

toga A loose outer garment worn by the upper classes in ancient Rome. A toga consisted of a large piece of cloth draped round the body.

63

Index